THE ALPHABET WAR

A Story about Dyslexia

Diane Burton Robb

pictures by
Gail Piazza

Albert Whitman & Company
Chicago, Illinois

To Alex, who can–DBR

To my daughter, Rachel–my creative inspiration.
Also, thanks to Cindy McGrellis for her valuable artistic vision.
And a very special thank-you to Theo and Orion
for being two very good Adams!–GP

Library of Congress Cataloging-in-Publication Data

The Alphabet War : a story about dyslexia / Diane Burton Robb ; illustrated by Gail Piazza.
p. cm.
Summary: Learning to read is a great struggle for Adam, but with expert help, hard work,
and belief in himself, he wins "The Alphabet War." Includes information about dyslexia.
1. Dyslexia—Fiction. 2. Schools—Fiction
I. Piazza, Gail. Ill. I. Title.
LCCN 2003017533
CIP
AC

Text copyright © 2004 by Diane Burton Robb
Pictures copyright © 2004 by Gail Piazza
Hardcover edition published in 2004 by Albert Whitman & Company
Paperback edition published in 2017 by Albert Whitman & Company
ISBN 978-0-8075-0304-1

Printed in China
10 9 8 7 6 5 4 3 2 1 LP 22 21 20 19 18 17

The illustrations were created in pastel.

For more information about Albert Whitman & Company,
visit our website at www.albertwhitman.com.

A Note for Parents and Teachers

Adam, who has dyslexia, is not alone when he wanders off into the ozone to escape what is for him the difficult task of learning to read. Like Adam, there are many children with learning disabilities in schools today. Such a child may begin school full of excitement and eager to learn to read. Over time, with failure after failure, that enthusiasm erodes, and the student goes off into his or her own world.

How many times have parents and teachers thought that if children would just try harder, they could succeed! But Adam's difficulty is not brought on by a lackadaisical attitude. Students with learning disabilities can try and try and try, until learning to read and spell becomes a real war. Too often they lose the fight. Sometimes they are so frustrated they misbehave. While parents should not use a learning disability as an excuse for not trying or for disruptive behavior, they should understand the difficult challenges their child faces.

It is important for parents to find the strengths in their sons and daughters by giving them the opportunities to participate in many different kinds of activities. Some children with learning disabilities perform well in math or science, in sports, or the arts. Parents and teachers should help shine the spotlight on these talents.

The good news is that children with learning disabilities can get help. When children who are at risk for reading failure are identified as early as possible (and this can be done as early as kindergarten and definitely by the end of first grade), intensive, explicit, systematic, and multisensory instruction can be provided. Students may not become speed readers, but, like Adam, they can win the Alphabet War.

For more information and resources, contact the Learning Disabilities Association of America (www.ldaamerica.org) or the International Dyslexia Association (www.dyslexiaida.org).

James O. Grant, PhD
Professor of Education
Grand Valley State University
Grand Rapids, Michigan

When Adam was little, he loved to sink into his mother's warm lap and listen to her read.

He would close his eyes and imagine himself crouching behind a huge saltshaker as a terrible voice thundered, "Fee-fi-fo-fum!"

His mother could just look at the pages of "Jack and the Beanstalk" and suddenly know how the beanstalk shuddered and swayed under the weight of the angry giant.

I can't do that, thought Adam.

But he didn't care. At preschool, he and his best friend, Walter, headed straight for the monkey bars and pretended they were shinnying down the beanstalk with the golden goose.

When Adam and Walter were five, they started kindergarten. Their teacher, Mrs. Brown, gathered the children in a circle and opened a book. Adam closed his eyes and listened to the *swish-swish* of pages being turned and imagined he was a mouse asking for a glass of milk.

Mrs. Brown wanted the class to learn about letters. Adam tried hard to learn their names. But *b* and *d* looked too much alike. So did *p* and *q*.

"I can't do that," he said to himself. But he didn't care much. He liked to color. He molded clay. He learned new songs.

By the end of the year, he'd learned enough letters to write his first and last name. Walter knew all the letters.

In first grade, Adam's new teacher wanted everyone to start putting the letters into words. Mrs. Small wanted them to read!

"We can do that," said a few children.

Mrs. Small smiled. "You can all do that," she said. "And you all will very soon."

That was the beginning of the Alphabet War. Every day, Adam sat at his desk and watched letters parading up and down, back and forth, all around the edges of the room. There were words on cards, words dangling on strings, words clipped together like necklaces, big words, little words, black words, blue words, green words, yellow words.

He tried to pay attention. But *was* looked like *saw*. And why did Mrs. Small say *cat* had three sounds, when Adam heard only one, as quick as the crack of a stick?

He was happy when it was time for gym.

Every day, Mrs. Small showed the class a different card with letters on it and asked them what it said. By Halloween, Adam was one of the few children who didn't call out the answer.

And he was trying hard! But he still read *then* when everyone else read *there*. The letters fluttered in his head like moths trapped in a jar.

One day in late winter, Adam found a way to shut out the Alphabet War. He closed his eyes and put his head on his desk. He listened to the swirl of words and the *clink-clank* of the heat vent and imagined himself battling a bristling army of *d*'s marching over a hill.

A few minutes later, Mrs. Small stood in front of his desk, tapping her foot.

She pointed to a card and asked him what it said.

"I can't do that," said Adam quietly.

"You can do that," said Mrs. Small. But she wasn't smiling.

At the end of first grade, Adam's parents hired a special teacher, called a tutor, to help him learn to read during the summer. She made charts of all the vowel sounds for him to learn.

He tried, but most of the time the insides of words got mixed up anyway. How could *two* and *too* sound the same but look different? Why did *eight* start with *e* and *ate* start with *a*?

After a while, he stopped listening.

He pretended he was being held prisoner in the castle of an evil king, who tormented him with vowels.

In second grade, he found out that he didn't just have to read and write. He had to spell!

He could tell his class how Abe Lincoln fought off five river pirates. He could slam a hockey puck as far as Brinks's garage. He could add and subtract. But he still couldn't point to the letter *w* and make the right sound. And he certainly couldn't spell.

For spelling tests, it helped a little if he tried to memorize the words by shape. *Book* looked like a locomotive. *Well* looked like a gate left open. He only got a few words right, and he hardly ever remembered how to spell them afterward.

By spring, only two people in his class hadn't started the second grade reader. On Tuesdays and Thursdays, Adam and Ashley left the classroom for extra practice with a reading helper. At first, everybody stared.

"Kindergarten baby!" chanted Joshua at recess.

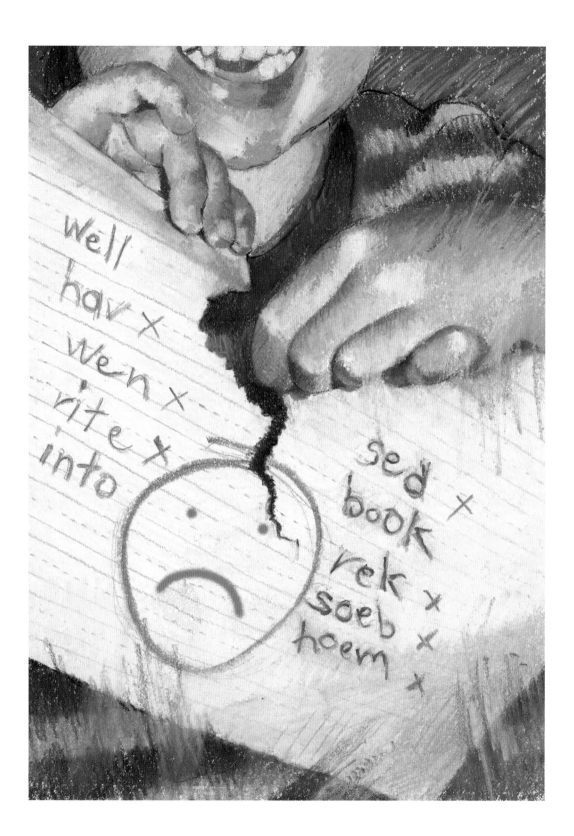

Adam kicked him and got
sent to the principal's office.

By the end of second grade, Adam knew it was hopeless.

Walter could read a two-hundred-page chapter book. Adam couldn't read the directions at the top of a math paper. When he looked at the signs posted all over the room, he felt like he was on the planet Neptune. During reading group, he watched a fly bumping against the window. He bothered other kids. He kicked the wall.

Most of the time, Adam sat at his desk and pretended.

But when he started third grade, he found out that pretending wasn't going to be enough.

His teacher, the principal, his parents, and some other grown-ups he didn't even know got together and made a plan. Adam's dad explained they were going to find out which way he learned best.

Soon after that, a man with round glasses and a kind voice asked a lot of questions and sat with him while he took a long test. The man told him not to worry because it was the kind of test you couldn't pass or fail. But Adam didn't believe him.

He felt like a bug under a microscope.

Now Adam had a teacher all to himself to help with reading, writing, and spelling. Mrs. Wood explained that the test showed he was very smart, but the part of his brain that should help figure out letters and sounds and turn them into words just wasn't working, like a space station cut off from mission control. She said all he had to do to learn how to read was fix the connection.

"I can't do that," said Adam wearily. He didn't believe her. Anyway, how could he be smart when there were first graders who could read better than he could?

"You *can* do that," said Mrs. Wood. "But it will take time."

Adam wasn't so sure.

Mrs. Wood explained that reading was like knowing a secret code. If you learned the sounds and patterns the letters made, you could break the code.

She started teaching Adam to read all over again. She broke the words apart into smaller pieces. She showed him what letters sounded like alone and together. Sometimes they traced words in a tray of sand or wrote them in different colors. Adam learned how to keep the letters apart by saying each sound out loud as he tapped on his arm.

It helped, a little. But often a word Adam knew on one page would be gone by the next, like a snowflake melting in the palm of his hand.

By spring, Adam could read a little better. He had to remember to look carefully at the insides of words and listen hard inside his head.

But Mrs. Wood was right. Most of the time, *if* he remembered the letter sounds and *if* he remembered the rules (and he didn't always remember), he could figure out what the word said. But whenever he saw a whole page full of words, they buzzed like angry bees, and he had to look away.

"I can't do that," said Adam.

"You can do that," said his mother. "Believe in yourself."

Summer came. Adam mowed the lawn, spent money on candy at the corner store (and could count his own change), built another fort in the backyard with Walter, and went to summer camp, just like the other kids.

When Adam started fourth grade in September, everyone else in reading class seemed to flit from word to word like hummingbirds. To him, words were like boulders. He had to climb over them, one by one.

One day, his teacher gave the class a test on magnets. Adam knew all about magnets. But he couldn't read the questions.

He was surprised when Mr. Chase called him over and read the questions out loud. He answered them. Almost perfectly.

Later, Mr. Chase set up a demonstration on conductors. He asked if anyone could position the wires to turn on the light bulb. Adam could. He went up to the model, connected the wires, and the light went on. The whole class cheered.

Adam was surprised. Maybe he was smarter than he thought. From then on, he took chances, even when he was afraid to be wrong. Sometimes he was. But lots of times, he was right.

Once he stopped noticing everything he couldn't do, he began to see everything he could. He could stand up in front of the class and give a perfect oral report, especially about hockey. He knew scary things about Blackbeard that made even Walter squirm. From an old pair of skates and a piece of wood, he could put together a skateboard that could whip anybody racing down Third Street Hill.

He wasn't dumb. He was just a different kind of thinker. Now whenever he had to read and the letters whinnied and bucked and wouldn't stand still, he lassoed them one by one and lined them up until he knew what they said. It wasn't easy. It never would be. Sometimes just listening was better.

One day, his mother gave him a book about pirates. He felt the boom of the cannon as the ship pitched and tossed in the howling sea.

Suddenly he stopped. He realized he was alone, reading to himself.

"I can do this," said Adam.

And he could.